THE LITTLE BOOK OF

Dragons

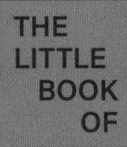

THE
LITTLE
BOOK
OF

Dragons

Carolyne Larrington

BRITISH LIBRARY

First published in 2025 by

The British Library

96 Euston Road

London NW1 2DB

ISBN 978 0 7123 5558 2

Cataloguing-in Publication Data
A catalogue record for this book is available from the
British Library

Title page: T. H. Robinson's 1905 illustration of the Red-Crosse
Knight and the Dragon, from *Una and the Red Cross Knight and
Other Tales from Spenser's Faery Queene.*

Designed and typeset by Georgie Hewitt
Picture Research by Sally Nicholls

Printed and bound in the Czech Republic by PBTisk

For product safety information, please visit shop.bl.uk/pages/
british-library-publishing, or the Publishing pages on bl.uk.

CONTENTS

Tab. XII.

Draco bipes apteros captus in
Agro Bononiensi.

Draco alatus Apes
ex Gremio Aldro.

Figura ex Pareo.

INTRODUCTION

Dragons are among the most fearsome monsters in the Western legendarium. Whether they breathe fire or spit poison or crush beasts and people in their snaky coils, they are tricky to deal with. Many of them are effectively armoured against attack, so that the hero must guess where their vulnerable spot is. They arrive in a neighbourhood from who knows where and annoy the inhabitants: some are attracted by unguarded hoards of gold; some are exceptionally wise, imparting mysterious lore; and some are just a nuisance. In this book we will meet many dragons from the Western tradition, in stories that originate in prehistoric times, and chart the emergence of the medieval dragon who lurks in the pages of romances, bestiaries, saints' lives and travel accounts. Dragons have many cousins in world mythology, where they symbolise very different energies from the hostile, avaricious, even diabolical figures of the Western tradition: they are creative and fertile, bringing good fortune as well as embodying wisdom and power. Along the way we will discover the various methods of overcoming the dragons whose depredations oppress their

Types of dragons from *Historiae naturalis de quadrupedibus*, 1657.

neighbourhoods – some heroic, some less so. In the West, dragons move into local folklore, where their deeds are recorded in balladry, and then, with the revival of interest in medieval literature in the nineteenth century, into children's stories, where they can be tamed, even domesticated. With the emergence of fantasy as a key popular genre, dragons have a significant role to play in some of the best-known Secondary Worlds of modern media franchises, and these dragons have captured the imaginations of people all over the world.

What is a dragon?

Dragons are, broadly speaking, monsters in reptilian form. They vary considerably in size: they are mostly very large – indeed the dragons in HBO's *Game of Thrones* are as colossal as Boeing 747 aeroplanes – and they are almost always big enough to give a hero pause. In some medieval illustrations, they can appear no larger than medium-sized dogs (a question of perspective). Dragons come in several varieties. Some have wings, and this type usually spouts fire. Others are wingless and legless, creeping across the land in a serpentine fashion and often called 'worms' or 'lindworms.' Some dragons prowl on clawed legs, four, or sometimes two; others lurk in streams, rivers or the ocean. Here they threaten ships, but can also emerge to devour their prey on land. They may have multiple heads (seven is a favourite number, thanks to the seven-headed dragon from the biblical Book of Revelation), tails that also end in a head, and quite often horns.

In medieval bestiaries, dragons are considered a member of the class of serpents, and are lumped in with lizards, asps, vipers and a kind of Nile crocodile. The wyvern is considered a kind of dragon: a lizard-like beast, two-legged and winged, but not fire-breathing. A basilisk is a small serpent with a crest that looks like a crown: it kills with a single glance and spews poison. The cockatrice is a kind of wyvern with the head of a cockerel, also with a fatal glance; the two terms are often used interchangeably. Both kinds of creature can be killed by throwing a weasel into their lair; the smell of the weasel is deadly, while the cockatrice perishes if shown its own reflection. Finally, the chimaera is a part-dragon hybrid; her hindquarters are dragonish, her middle section that of a goat, and she has a lion's head, from which she spouts flames.

Whether sea-serpents are dragons is an interesting question. Clearly the fiery type of dragon will not thrive in a watery environment, but the natural habitat of East Asian dragons is the river. Some varieties of sea-serpent can spit poison, such as the Great Sea-Serpent spotted near Greenland by the Danish-Norwegian missionary Hans Egede in the eighteenth century; this is a feature that makes them rather more dragon-like. Other dragons or worms are not really monsters at all. They turn out to be enchanted humans, and heroes who are brave and resourceful enough can rescue them from their hideous fates.

Overleaf: Illustrations from a 1595 copy of *Historia animalium* showing (clockwise from top left) cerastes, basilisk, natrix and jaculus serpents.

114
CERASTES

IACULUS
115
CHALCIDA

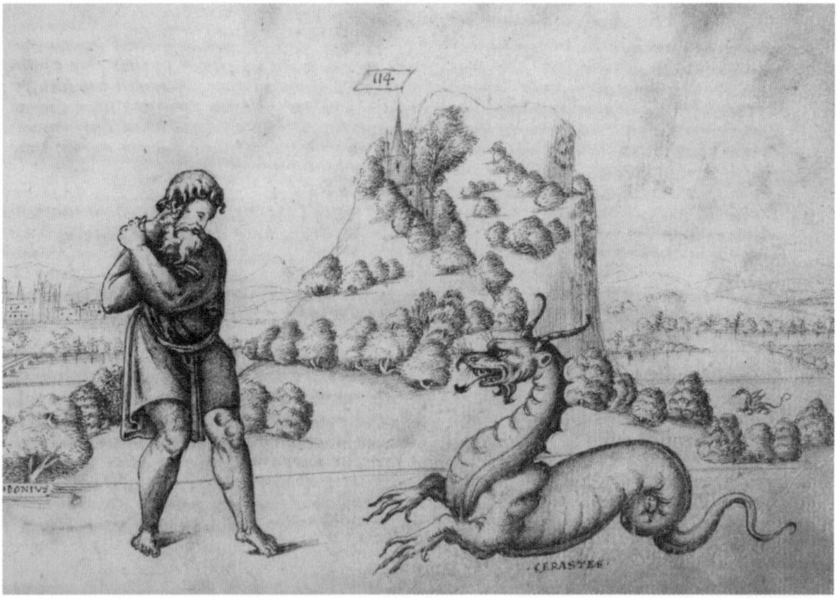

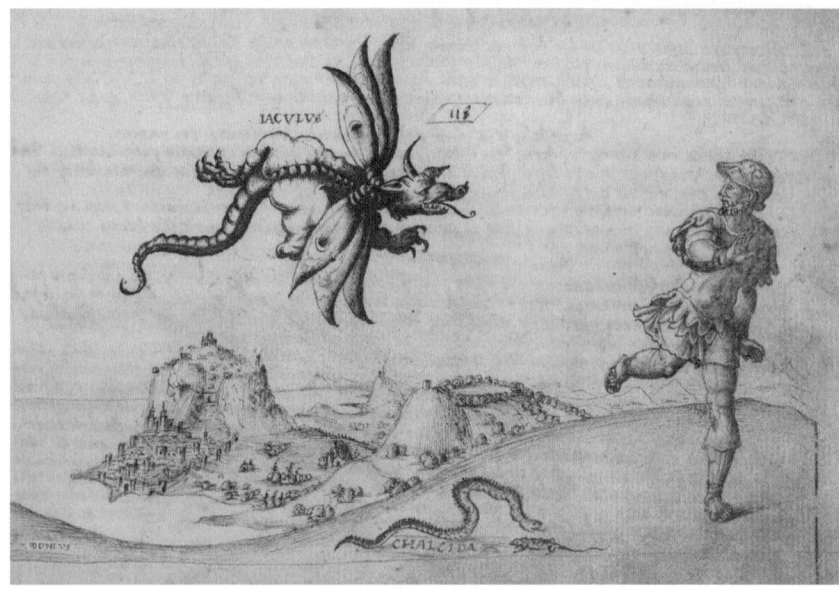

130

Basilisco

BASILISCVS

IDONIVS

REGVLVS
BASILISCVS

117

NATRIX

ONIVS

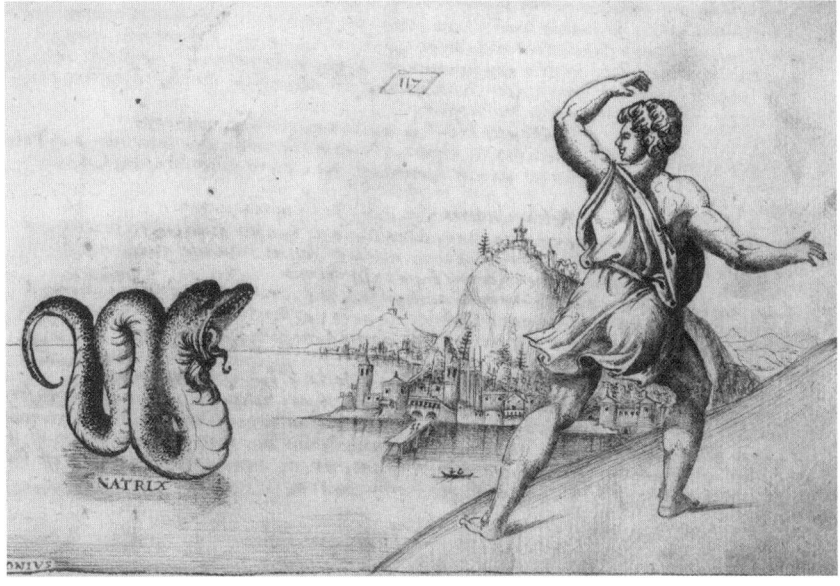

The daughter of the dragon-king Ryūo drawing a bucket from a well encircled by a dragon, from an Edo-period woodblock print by Totoya Hokkei.

The Origins of Dragons

No theory that has been suggested so far adequately accounts for the plethora of tales about dragons and other snake-monsters around the world. At one time it seemed plausible that tales about dragons originated in fossil finds: what were dinosaurs if not different kinds of dragon? But there are plenty of tales from areas without significant fossil finds. More persuasive, perhaps, is the theory that our earliest ancestors' fear of snakes generated tales of monster-serpents which had an adaptive function: warning people to avoid all kinds of snakes, and embodying humans' enduring fear of such creatures. But the reasons for the occurrence of dragon-tales all across the world remain unresolved. One fact is certain, however: the dragon does not preserve a vestigial memory of humans' encounters with dinosaurs. Dinosaurs were extinct millions of years before we humans evolved from our distant mammalian ancestors.

Dragons have complex symbolic functions in both traditional and modern stories. They are sometimes regarded as just another strange beast, living mostly in distant habitats. Such creatures may be unpleasant and dangerous but there are methods for overcoming them. Other dragons are regarded as the embodiment of evil, the ultimate foe for the supreme hero to battle with: thereby he proves his courage and is acclaimed for his unmatched prowess. It is said of the Norse hero Sigurd, who slew the dragon Fáfnir, that he was honoured as the greatest of heroes all across Northern Europe and that his fame would endure as long as the world lasts. From symbol of evil, it is a short step to dragons becoming an actual manifestation of the Devil in the European tradition, appearing in terrifying form to inflict misery on humans and cause them to doubt their Christian faith. Not all dragons fall into these categories; in East Asia they are auspicious creatures, wise and benevolent, bringing fertility to the land through their power over water. Elsewhere in the world the dragon or serpent symbolises a creative, generative force essential to human well-being.

Salv. Rosa inv.   C.F. Holtzmann fec. 1765.

JASON.

DRAGONS OF THE ANCIENT WORLD

Chaos-Monsters from India and the Ancient Near East

Tales of the monster-killing hero are very ancient indeed, although the foe is not always clearly identified as definitively dragon-like in form. In the ancient Sanskrit *Rig Veda*, the god Indra kills Vritra with a specially forged weapon. Vritra's name means 'the one who covers'; he is the demon of drought and prevents access to the rivers of the world. He is described as having neither hands nor feet, and he hisses and snorts terrifyingly: key dragon characteristics. Ahi, sometimes said to be his brother, also has a rain-denying function, and is consistently described as a monstrous serpent.

An eighteenth-century print by Carl Friedrich Holtzmann depicting the dragon of Colchis overcome by the Greek hero Jason.

In the ancient Near East, we find other monstrous dragon-like creatures. In the Babylonian creation epic, the *Enūma Elish*, Tiamat is a terrifying female figure with serpentine features, the embodiment of the sea. She mates with Apsu, who signifies the groundwaters, and gives birth to the first generation of gods. Tiamat is slain by the god Marduk, who uses the winds to inflate and explode her body; her remains are subsequently used to construct the world. In Egyptian myth, Ra, the sun-god, battles with Apep, the god of chaos in serpent form, every night when the sun passes below the horizon into the underworld. Rituals of various kinds are required in the human world to secure the sun's daily return. Myths from the Indo-European language family, which includes Sanskrit, Greek, Latin and the Romance, Germanic and Celtic languages, has its fair share of such monsters, confronting divine or semi-divine heroes; their triumph symbolises the victory of creative order over primeval chaos. One of the best-known is the Old Norse Jörmungandr, the Midgardsormr or World-Serpent. Child of the god Loki, this creature is flung into the outer ocean by the gods, where it grows huge, girdling the earth and menacing those who sail out too far. When the day of *ragna rök* (the end of the world) comes, the World-Serpent will rise from the depths and do battle against the god Thor. Although the god will smash its skull with his famous hammer, as Thor turns away victorious, he will stagger only nine paces before he falls dead, slain by the serpent's venomous spittle.

Greek myth has a good number of dragons and serpentine monsters. Zeus, king of the gods, fights against Typhon, who lurks

Illustration of a bas-relief depicting an Assyrian god fighting a dragon-like monster, often associated with the battle of Marduk against Tiamat, 865–860 BCE.

underground, has a hundred snake heads and is at least partly humanoid. Zeus overcomes him in a battle on a cosmic scale before binding and imprisoning him under Mount Etna, marking his victory over primordial chaos. Typhon is not the only dragon whose fire is the origin of a volcano; Iceland owes its origins to the Mester Stoor Worm, according to Orkney legend. Other Greek dragons guard springs of water; they must be eliminated if the city which the hero intends to establish is to have an adequate water supply. So Cadmus, the legendary founder of Thebes, kills a dragon stationed by the Greek war-god Ares at a spring in order to build the city. Although Ares is offended by the killing of his sacred creature, he later gives Cadmus his daughter Harmonia in marriage. Ladon is the dragon who guards the golden apples of the Hesperides, slain by Heracles as one of his Twelve Labours, while the dragon of Colchis guards the Golden Fleece until Jason succeeds in stealing it (aided by Medea, who puts the beast to sleep with powerful drugs and incantations). These guardian-dragons find their echo in medieval legend, where similar creatures jealously watch over gold hoards.

Heracles also kills the many-headed Hydra, lurking in the Lernean marshes, as the second of his Twelve Labours; by dispelling the unhealthy miasma of the monster he makes the area habitable for humans. Python, early guardian of the famous shrine of Apollo at Delphi, was slain by Apollo while the god was still a child. The classical myths thus present a recurrent pattern: the monstrous serpent has often been appointed guardian of a sacred place by a god, but it has subsequently become a destructive force more widely in the land. It has an affinity with water, which it keeps from the humans who need it, and can only be overcome by a god or hero. Many of these classical dragon figures have multiple heads with serried rows of terrifying teeth; they also spew out poison, as liquid or vapour, or else breathe jets of fire just as do their later relatives.

Greek and Roman myth also knows a kind of sea-monster whose features contribute a good deal to the later Western image of the

Hercules slaying the hydra, from Jacopo Camphora's manuscript
De immortalitate animae, 1472.

ADEO FORTITVDO MEA

Candida cum toties referat uictoria palmas
In tua damna tibi quid iuuat esse feram.
Ille deus summum petet insuperatus olympu
Torrida lerneis flebis echidna uadis.

dragon. Less snaky, more whale-like, the *ketos* (source of our word *cetacean*) is the kind of monster that menaced the Greek princess Andromeda. Bound on the seashore to satisfy the monster's ravenous appetite for devouring young girls, Andromeda is rescued at the last moment by the hero Perseus, wearing his winged sandals. He had been sent to kill Medusa, the fearsome snake-haired female monster who could turn men to stone with a single glance; by using a mirror he had turned her petrifying powers back on herself. Now armed with Medusa's head, Perseus easily thwarts the sea-monster, which immediately turns to stone: the first dragon to become a landmark. A number of other water-dragons and sea-serpents will appear later in this book.

Leviathan and Other Biblical Dragons

The biblical Old Testament mentions a dragon-like monster called Leviathan, a kind of 'twisted serpent' or 'dragon-serpent' that lives in the depths of the sea, and to which God is hostile. In one psalm God is said to have crushed Leviathan's heads and fed his remains to the beasts of the desert. Another psalm reminds us, however, that God himself created Leviathan and set him to play in the ocean, while in the Book of Job, the creature functions as a symbol of God's power, invulnerable to attack as flames spout from its mouth and smoke from its nostrils. In later Christian thinking,

The *ketos* threatening Andromeda as Perseus hovers overhead, in a Roman fresco from the imperial villa at Boscotrecase, Pompeii.

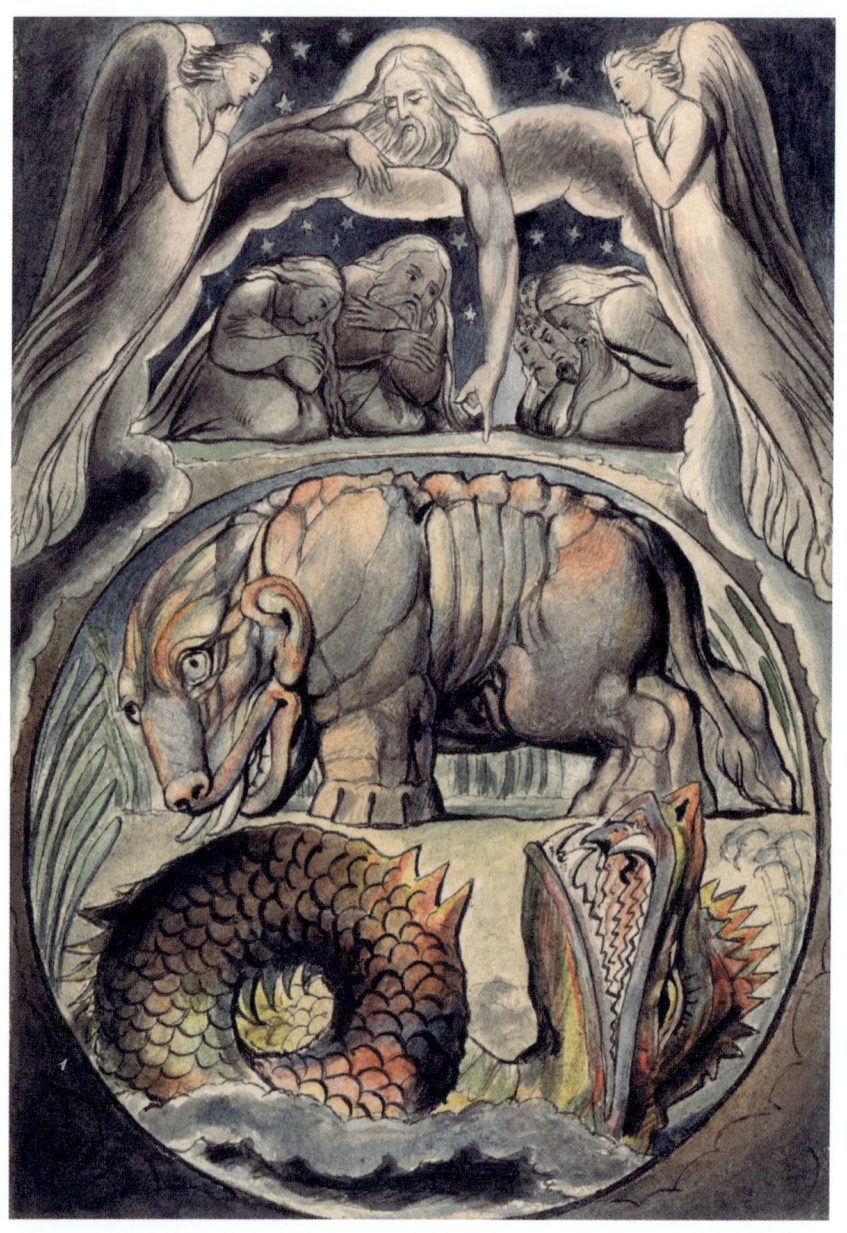

Leviathan becomes a figure for Satan; lines in the Book of Job in which God asks the suffering Job, 'Canst thou draw Leviathan with an hook? Or his tongue with a cord which thou lettest down?' were taken as referring to Jesus's death on the Cross. Unlike Job, who is helpless in the face of Satan's torments, Christ's sacrifice did indeed overthrow the power of the Devil over humankind.

The story of Bel and the Dragon in the biblical Apocrypha features the prophet Daniel as the clever hero – the earliest in that line of protagonists who overcome dragons through cunning, not brute strength or God's power. Challenged by the ruler of Babylon to confront a dragon that was worshipped by the people as a god, Daniel devises an enticing form of dragon-bait: pitch, fat and hair, boiled together and shaped into cakes. When the dragon devours the cakes, it explodes: the pitch presumably reacts badly with the monster's fiery interior. A similar tale is told of Alexander the Great in the tenth-century Persian epic, the *Shahnameh*, composed by the poet Ferdowsi. There Alexander disposes of a dragon by offering it cow-hides stuffed with poison and tar. We will see later how folk heroes often overcome dragons by devising an effective weapon, one which turns the monster's most deadly aspects against itself.

In the Book of Revelation in the New Testament, the seventh portent of the coming apocalypse is the appearance of a red dragon

Behemoth and Leviathan in a watercolour by John Linnell, after William Blake.

یار کند شتن بر ور سپاه

بسه شهر با او ندار با با تاو

بران نا تا نیا یدازین روی

نفرسود سالار را هیم جوی

بکشند کاو ی بر آکنده پوست

بدم پوستها را پر از باد کرد

جوزه چو یکی ابر فرفت ناب

جوگاه از سری کوه بندست

جرا ز پوست پوشش کنده شد

می و سرشش با بران کونک

همی دود ز هرش بر بابا با

خورش با نه ش شبی سنجگا

بپیچاند از ما کرو کرده

کز از وز نده هند چیزی با دوست

زدار نیکی رهنش یاد کرد

جبلان یکی ابر دیش یا

بران از دها دل نبر خشتند

بر اندام ز هرش پر آکنده

جنین نازمانی بر آمد درزک

همی دود زهرش بر بابا

هی آتش افروز داز کام

خریم و بران کوه خار با بریم

درم از رو سالار روی کنج

جوان اثر و بار هرش بد

با کند چوشش زهرو بینفت

نفرمود تا پوست بردند نزن

زبانش کبود و دوشش خون

فردیبرد جوب با و کاو از دها

همه رو کانیش سوراخ کرد

سپاهی ی بر و بر با با ریدیتیم

دو کیسو بود سل دایم

با ندیشه با دار ابرام

سباور باور شیش کاوح

زمردان لشکر کزین کرد

سوی اشه با روی بهنار

همی و شت بر دشت کنده

همی آتش آمد از که ش بهرو

جوا مذ رجک دلیران را

بغز شرش را کپستاخ کرد

سپای اندان که بجمبر کیه

with seven heads, ten horns, and seven crowns on its heads. War now breaks out in heaven: the archangel Michael and his band of angels fight against the dragon and the creature, along with his supporters, is cast down to earth for it is 'the ancient serpent, called Satan'. The dragon is hurled into the Abyss, its powers limited until the last times and the coming of the Antichrist, when it will be loosed once more. This satanic dragon delegates its power to two bizarre beasts: one resembles a leopard with bears' feet and a lion's mouth, and with the same number of heads and horns as the dragon. The second beast has 'a voice like a dragon' and two horns like a lamb. The Book of Revelation was often copied separately from the rest of the Bible, and its monsters were very frequently illustrated in the medieval period. Conceptions of the Revelation dragon change visibly over the centuries, as it gradually develops smaller, then larger, wings and a pair of legs, while its head becomes less reptilian and more animal-like. It gains ears, and has impressive horns (as mandated in Revelation) and quite often a vestigial beard. The identification of this Revelation dragon with Satan affects images of Adam and Eve in the Garden of Eden, too; in many depictions the tempting Serpent becomes less snake-like and distinctly dragonish in appearance.

Iskandar (Alexander) killing a dragon, from a manuscript of the epic poem *Shahnameh* by the Persian poet Ferdowsi.

Angels, led by the archangel Michael, fighting dragons in the Revelation
of St John, from the Val-Dieu Apocalypse manuscript.

Opposite: The satanic seven-headed dragon and the terrifying beast from
the sea in the Book of Revelation, as depicted in the Queen Mary Apocalypse,
fourteenth century.

...uilite establee par lour oreisons auertissent les tribulatons ge les
...rables enuirent. Ou en autre maniere par le elbe est signifie richesse
...u diables enuoit astime sont en seinte Eglise qui il ne la poet
...estruire par tribulacion. Mes la terre ourt sa bouche, ceo sont siu
...uettous qi transflatent les richesses, si ge siu don fiz de seinte egl
...renuissent en pourete et de nuit gard. ¶ Ceo ge siu dragon se tour
...na uers la femine et sen ala combatre ouo les autres de son linage
...gnisie come auant ge qui il est suilli as oeus de haute uie il se
...rent a plusbas qi oint sa fei et ciel et se gardent de pecchie mortel
...de ceux ne uient il fors com Et ceus sont signifiez par la gnele
...de la mer ou il se assist.

cum dr̄. q̄cq̄d labr̄ dūm tenet̄. ut pīscit̄ serpens. Serpens au͞
nom̄ accipit̄ q̄a occultis accessib̄; serpit̄. n̄ apt̄is passib̄; s̄ squa
maḡ minutissimis nisib̄; reptit̄. Illa au͞ que q̄uior pedib̄; ni
tunt̄ur. sic̄ lacerte. & stilliones. n̄ serpentes s̄ reptilia nom̄
nant̄. Serpentes aut̄ reptilia t̄o que uentre & pectore
reptant̄. Quorū tot uenena: q̄t genera. tot pnicies. tot
dolores. q̄t colores habent̄ur. Draco.

Draco maior cunctorum serpentium siue omniū
animantium sr̄ tram. Hunc greci draconta uocant.
unde & diriuatū e͂ inlatinū. ut draco diceret̄ur.
Qui sepe ab speluncis abstract̄ fert̄ inaere͂. concitat̄q̄;

BESTIARY DRAGONS

Medieval bestiaries are usually richly illustrated Latin accounts of the natures and symbolic meanings of animals. They draw upon late classical lore such as the third-century CE *Physiologus* and the encyclopedic work, *Etymologiae*, compiled by the sixth- to seventh-century writer Isidore of Seville, who regarded the dragon as just as real as a lion or frog. Alongside mammals, fish and birds, the bestiaries depict different kinds of serpentine beasts, discussing their habits and sometimes attributing allegorical significance to them. We met some of these creatures earlier, such as the basilisk and cockatrice; to them can be added such obscure reptiles as the asp that blocks its ear with its tail so as to be immune to snake-charmers, and the boa, prevalent in Italy, that kills cattle by sucking much too much milk from cows' udders. The greatest of all serpents, though, is the dragon. Its deadliest weapon is not its teeth nor its claws, but rather its lashing tail and powerful coils. It particularly hates elephants and lurks near their habitats to suffocate them; this apparently is why elephants give birth in water where the dragon dares not come. The dragon

A dragon overpowering an elephant in a thirteenth-century bestiary.

eius illabi. Cocodrillus q subito uiuum eum truglu
tit. Ille ut dilanians omnia uiscera eius no solu uiuus
sed etiam penitus illesus. Sic ergo mors & infernus figuram
hint cocodrilli. quorum mimici. e. dns ihc xpc. Nã assu
mens humanã carnem. descendit ad infernum. & disrum
pens omnia uiscera eius. eduxit eos q iuste tenebantur
ab eo. Mortificauit enim ipsã mortem. resurgens ex mor
tuis. & illi insultat ppha dicens. O mors ero mors tua.
morsus tuus ero inferne.

Boas.

Boas anguis italie immẽ
sa mole psequit greges
armtor & bubalos. &
plurimo lacte irriguis se ubi
bus innectit. & sugens inimit
atq; inde a boum de populati
one boas nomen accepit. Iaculus.

Iaculus serpens uolans.
De quo lucanus. Iaculiq;
uolantes exiliunt. ++. in arboribz & du aliqd animal om
um fuerit. iactant se sup eu & puniunt. Vnde & iaculi
dicti sunt.
In arabia
autẽ serpentes albi sũ cũ alis. que syrene uocant. que
plus currunt ab eqs. sz etiã & uolare dicunt. quorum tñ
uirus. e. ut morsu ante mors insequat quã dolor. Seps.

is terrified of panthers, whose sweet breath it finds unbearable. Bestiary dragons do not breathe fire; rather, the venom spurting from their mouths gives the appearance of flames. Medieval scholars add further dragon-lore. They can be caught and ridden, says Thomas of Cantimpré, but if made to cross large expanses of sea they are likely to tire and plunge into the ocean. Thomas also gives a foolproof method for killing dragons: a calf carcass stuffed with quicklime. When the dragon ingests it, the quicklime causes a great thirst, but when the beast slakes its thirst with water the ensuing chemical reaction will destroy it.

Since these dragons are conceived of as actual, if exotic, animals, their body parts have magical and medicinal purposes. Taken neat, dragon's blood is instantly fatal, and its other body parts are noxious. For those plagued by ghosts and goblins at night, a concoction made of the tongue, eyes, gall and intestines of a dragon, boiled in wine, is efficacious if the victim is anointed with the liquid. The dragon's brain contains a valuable white stone, but it dissolves if extracted after the dragon is dead. And, according to Hildegard of Bingen, a thoroughly diluted solution of dragon's blood will break up gall- or kidney-stones.

Cattle are attacked by the boa, a kind of winged serpent,
in a thirteenth-century bestiary.

More Allegorical Dragons

The bestiary writers agree that the dragon represents the Devil, lying in wait for humans (or elephants) and seeking to ensnare them in his snaky coils. The watery habitat where elephants give birth figures Christian baptism, while the panther with his sweet breath is Jesus Christ who can drive the Devil away. In the first book of Sir Edmund Spenser's late sixteenth-century allegorical poem, *The Faerie Queene*, the Red-Crosse Knight sallies forth with the lady Una (signifying the true Anglican Church) to do battle against a terrible she-dragon, Errour, whose monstrous body produces endless offspring that must also be killed. Even when she is beheaded, she generates further horror: her progeny drink her blood and devour her, until 'their bellies swolne … with fulnesse burst' and they all perish. This is not the only dragon that the Red-Crosse Knight faces. At the end of Book One, now in Una's homeland, he encounters a winged dragon, armoured in impenetrable scales, with fiery eyes, huge claws and three ranks of iron teeth. At the end of the first day's fighting the dragon ill-advisedly hurls the knight into a nearby well; this is the 'well of life', from which he emerges next morning ready to do battle again. Finally, on the third day of the combat, as the dragon's jaws gape to devour him, the knight thrusts his sword deep into its innards and the monster perishes. Spenser's dragon-fight is elaborated from the semi-allegorical dragon-fight of Bevis of Hampton, discussed below in 'Creeping Dragons.'

The Red-Crosse Knight, watched by Lady Una, does battle against the she-dragon Errour, in a seventeenth-century edition of *The Faerie Queene*.

FLYING AND FIERY DRAGONS

The earliest dragons recorded in Britain are flying, fire-breathing beasts: fire-drakes. There is a note in *The Anglo-Saxon Chronicle* for the ill-fated year 793, recording that fiery dragons were spotted in the skies over Northumbria before the Vikings raided the monastery on the island of Lindisfarne: an omen of the dark times to come as the country fell victim to more and more attacks from the Scandinavian pirates in their dragon-prowed ships. Old English poetry mentions the habits of dragons quite casually: the dragon is wise and lies on its treasure in its mound, we learn in the *Cotton Maxims*; in *Beowulf*, dragons, old and wise, are said to seek out heathen gold to guard. In a short, fragmentary battle-poem, some warriors who are taken by surprise in a night-time assault realise that the advancing lights they can see are torches carried by the enemy, not, as they might first think, a dragon flying from the east.

Dragon Awakens by Theodor Kittelsen, 1903.

Beowulf's Dragon

The dragon in the Old English poetic masterpiece, *Beowulf*, is the best-known of these early monsters. This dragon flies and spews out both flames and poison. It arrives in the vicinity of King Beowulf's hall in Geatland (in southern Sweden) and makes its home in a barrow, a human construction that houses a long-forgotten treasure hoard. The dragon becomes the guardian of the hoard and rests peacefully on top of it until a slave finds his way into the lair and steals a goblet from the pile of gleaming gold. This loss arouses the dragon's fury; it waits until nightfall, then takes to the air, wheeling through the skies and incinerating the settlement and the king's hall, symbol of his power. This speaks to a degree of instinctive intelligence on the dragon's part; not only does it notice when a single item from its huge hoard is missing, but it also identifies the king's hall and the surrounding dwellings as a worthy target for its vengeance.

Beowulf must act, and fast. He commissions an iron shield – for the standard wooden one would be useless – and considers whether to attack the dragon with a band of men. But he decides instead to face the monster single-handed, and, guided by the slave whose theft awakened the dragon's wrath in the first place, he enters the barrow and attacks. Beowulf's great sword fails against the dragon's armoured skin, and the hero is nearly overcome by its

The death of Beowulf and the dragon, illustrated by Henry Justice Ford in *The Red Book of Animal Stories*.

The death of BEOWULF

A longship with dragon prow from a Latin/Old English miscellany,
eleventh–twelfth century.

poisonous breath. His young kinsman, Wiglaf, comes at last to his
aid and together they kill the creature, apparently by piercing it in
the belly, while Beowulf manages to cut through its middle. The
dragon dies, but so too does Beowulf, succumbing to the beast's
poison. The king has a splendid funeral that honours his heroic
feats and his people consign the hard-won hoard back into the
earth once more. The dragon is tipped unceremoniously over a cliff
into the sea, but the poet laments that never again would people
see it 'playing in the sky in the middle of the night.' Slaying the
dragon is usually the culminating act in a young hero's career in
early medieval literature; *Beowulf* is unusual in that its hero is an
aged warrior, whose battle with the dragon turns out to be fatal.

Old Norse Dragons

The most significant Old Norse dragon is Fáfnir, a serpent-like creature (we will meet him, along with other 'Creeping Dragons', below). Most dragons found in Old Norse saga and romance can fly, and they are often fiery too. In one saga, a lad called Ketill, disregarding his father's warnings, sets off after sunset one evening northwards from his home. Suddenly he spots a flying creature, 'with coils and a tail like a snake, and wings like a dragon. Fire flashed from his eyes and jaws'. The dragon attacks Ketill who, after a struggle, manages to kill it with his axe. When he goes home, his father asks whether his disobedient boy happened to see any dangerous creatures while out. Ketill coolly remarks that he did in fact see a very sizeable fish and hacked it in half; he reckons it was probably the biggest female salmon ever fished at that lake. Ketill's father is impressed that his normally idle son has achieved this feat, saying that not many folk would compare the creature to a smallish fish. From now on Ketill will have the nickname 'salmon'.

Níðhögg, the dragon who lurks at the foot of the World-Tree, Yggdrasill, gnawing at its roots, seems like a serpentine dragon, for he keeps company with a knot of serpents. Yet after *ragna rök* (the end of the world), so the poem *The Seeress's Prophecy* tells us, when the new world has come into being, the dragon is seen flying across the sky, bearing corpses in his wings. Whether this signifies that dragonish evil is at work in the new world too, or whether Níðhögg is simply helping to tidy things up, is not clear: his continuing existence may owe something to the Dragon of Revelation.

The *Letter of Prester John* was a document purporting to have been sent by the legendary Christian ruler who was thought, from the twelfth century onwards, to hold sway in India. The *Letter* was supposedly sent to the Emperor of Byzantium to tell him that Christianity had a foothold beyond the Muslim lands, and that his country was one of untold riches and wonders. A forgery probably concocted by a European monk, the *Letter* drew upon the tradition of the Wonders of the East and the travels of Alexander the Great for its information. In one version, Prester John writes that among the marvels of his land are dragons that men could tame and then ride like horses. This 'fact' is reported in a mid-thirteenth-century Norwegian text and the practicality of the dragon as

The dragon Nídhögg gnawing on the roots of the World-Tree, together with other serpents, in a seventeenth-century Icelandic manuscript.

steed is treated with some scepticism. Clearly, dragon-riders, like those in George R. R. Martin's imagined world, are by no means a modern invention; medieval encyclopedia writers also regarded them as possible modes of transport. We saw earlier that Thomas of Cantimpré thought dragon-riding to be feasible.

Folkloric Flying Dragons

British folklore does not have many flying dragons, though some of its serpentine worms breathe fire instead of spitting poison. In the Exe valley, a fire-breathing dragon flies between two Iron Age hillforts, Dolbury Hill at Killerton and Cadbury Castle near Bickleigh. It guards the treasure buried within the two hills and, unusually, it is apparently still alive, its survival guaranteed by constantly moving between one hoard and the other so that it is never cornered by a treasure-seeking hero.

The aerial fiery terror unleashed by the *Beowulf*-monster would strike a powerful chord with J. R. R. Tolkien. In his essay 'On Fairy-Stories', he wrote, 'I desired dragons with a profound desire. Of course I, in my timid body, did not wish to have them in the neighbourhood.' As a professor of Old English and Old Norse literature, Tolkien was naturally very knowledgeable about dragons; thus he adapted the features of the *Beowulf*-dragon for his unforgettable creation, Smaug, the fearsome monster in *The Hobbit*. Like his Old English predecessor Smaug sits on a treasure hoard, flies and spouts flames, attacking the human settlement of Laketown, until he is finally shot down by Bard the Bowman. Smaug also talks – a trait borrowed from Fáfnir in the Old Norse *Saga of the Völsungs*. And Smaug, in turn, is the ancestor of George R. R. Martin's multitude of fire-breathing flying dragons, brought to the world's TV screens through HBO's shows *Game of Thrones* and *House of the Dragon*. The fame of these monsters has provoked a good deal of interest in fire-drakes and how they can be neutralised or defeated.

Fire-drakes are the most difficult of monsters to deal with once their anger is roused. If they are left alone with their gold, they do not tend to pose a threat to humankind, but when provoked they wreak much more damage than their creeping, poison-spitting cousins, destroying whole settlements and their populations. They cannot be appeased with cattle or maidens and restoring their stolen treasure is near-impossible. In medieval Europe, the flying fiery dragon symbolised the fear of sudden attack under cover of night and the horror of being trapped by your foes in a burning hall. Similarly, the great modern fire-drakes, Smaug and the dragons of George R. R. Martin's world, speak to our profound contemporary dread of aerial warfare, bombing raids and missiles raining down from the sky. Only a very particular set of skills, secret knowledge or a fated weapon can destroy such powerful monsters and end their reigns of terror.

A fire-breathing dragon attacks a lion, from the Taymouth Book of Hours, fourteenth century.

Qe mon espirt e mon corps

Seient tutditz de un acord

Et de un volour taunt qʼ a la mort.

Qe par mon̄ corps tʼames ne face

Rien qʼ malme sy deplace

Tut puissaunt dieu ⁊ creatour

Vncore i ad le tierce amour

CREEPING DRAGONS

Most folkloric dragons are more serpentine than the fire-drake; as a consequence they are often called worms, from the Old English *wyrm* and the Old Norse *ormr*, meaning 'snake'. They are resolutely earth-bound. Some are equipped with two or four legs, and others glide along in a snake-like fashion; indeed some German lindworms can roll themselves up into a hoop and bowl along at speed. In addition to their poisonous breath they spew venom against their enemies. These creatures are more predatory than the fire-drake; when they take up residence in a neighbourhood they choke the local economy, devouring cattle and sheep, and when they progress to eating young girls, they disastrously compromise the community's future.

Dragons, Gold and Girls

The most famous Old Norse dragon, Fáfnir, is an exception to the usual worm-type. Fáfnir was originally a kind of anthropomorphic

The dragon Fafner (Fáfnir) guards his hoard of gold, illustrated by Arthur Rackham in a 1911 edition of *The Ring of the Niblung*.

being – whether a human, a giant or a dwarf is not clear in the sources. His two brothers are remarkable: Otr is a shape-changer and Regin a renowned smith. Three Norse gods happen across Otr in his otter form and Loki throws a stone at him, killing him. Loki skins the otter and that night, when the gods seek hospitality at a nearby hall, Loki shows off his acquisition. Unfortunately, it is Otr's family's hall, and his furious father demands compensation. Loki has to steal the gold of the dwarf, Andvari, who puts a curse on it; notwithstanding this peril, Otr's father demands all the gold, sufficient to cover the otter-skin. Once the gods have left, the family falls to quarrelling. Otr's brothers demand a share of the gold and when their father refuses, Fáfnir kills him. Then he transforms himself into a dragon and goes off to Gnita-heath where he broods over his hoard but otherwise does no particular mischief to travellers. Perhaps because he was once a man, Fáfnir can speak and he has great mythological wisdom. Fáfnir's surviving brother, Regin, meanwhile plots to avenge his father and, more importantly, to get his hands on the gold.

Regin is the foster-father of the hero Sigurd and eggs him on to kill Fáfnir. With his smithing skill, Regin forges a mighty sword for the young man and they make their way up to Gnita-heath. Regin retreats while Sigurd ponders how to attack. An old man (in fact the god Odin) approaches and advises him to dig a pit, cover it in branches and hide within it. When the dragon slithers down to the river to drink, Sigurd can stab it from below; the old man sensibly advises the digging of auxiliary pits to catch the creature's venom and poisonous blood. The plan is successful. The dragon is mortally wounded and as Fáfnir lies dying he imparts some useful advice to the hero, in particular warning him not to trust Regin. Regin sets Sigurd to roasting the dragon's heart over a fire; when the lad pokes it to see if it is done, he burns his finger and puts it in his mouth. Thus, it is he and not Regin who acquires the magical ability to understand the language of birds. Some nearby nuthatches urge Sigurd to kill Regin and to make his way to a nearby mountain-top where the Valkyrie Brynhildr is sleeping. Sigurd dispatches the sleeping smith and goes off with the hoard. In some versions of the story, he also bathes in Fáfnir's blood; this confers invulnerability upon him, except for the one spot – his Achilles' heel – where a leaf sticks to his back, protecting the skin there from the blood. This weakness will later be Sigurd's undoing.

The pit-ambush is an unusual and comparatively unheroic way of killing the dragon; it may echo contemporary medieval boar-hunting techniques, but the method is depicted in tenth-century carvings telling the Sigurd story in Sweden and the Isle of Man. In the Old English poem *Beowulf*, a dragon-slaying is attributed not to Sigurd, but to his father, Sigemund (as he is spelled in Old English). Sigemund's battle with the serpent anticipates Beowulf's at the end of the poem, but with a more successful outcome. He enters the dragon's cave singlehandedly, kills the beast with a sword-blow that transfixes it to the cave wall and departs with a vast amount of treasure. It seems likely that Sigemund's battle, conforming as it does to the archetypal dragon-fights of classical myth, is the original version. The Norse story has been adapted to fit with the origin story for the gold, a history of deception and murder, and to note Sigurd's kindred's bond with their patron, Odin. That Fáfnir can speak makes him exceptional among pre-modern dragons; he warns against complacency and trusting others too much, vital life lessons that Sigurd will fail to learn.

The composer Richard Wagner reworked and popularised the story of the gold and the dragon in his 1876 opera cycle, *Der Ring des Nibelungen*, which draws upon the Old Norse sagas and poems. The connection between dragons and gold is dissipated in British folklore (though, as we saw, the Exe valley dragon guards two hoards).

In another Norse saga, a little serpent is given as a birthday gift to young Princess Thora. She knows that she needs to place a new gold piece beneath it every day to make her pet grow and her doting father accedes to her request. By the time Thora is of an age to wed, the hoard is huge and so is the dragon. It has wound itself around her quarters and refuses to let anyone else go in or out, and it is consuming oxen at a considerable rate. Thora's father promises the gold and the girl to whoever can rid him of this pest. Ragnar Shaggy-breeches is a king's son who is equal to the task. He gets trousers made of sheep-fleece, coated with pitch and covered in sand. This is effective protection against the surge of poison that the dying worm vomits out as the hero stabs it with his spear. Ragnar weds Thora and takes possession of the serpent-

Sigurd kills Fafner (Fáfnir) as he goes to the river to drink, by Arthur Rackham in *The Ring of the Niblung*, 1911.

hoard. This is his first feat but, at least in his own saga, he is soon outshone by his heroic sons. Ragnar turns out to be a dragon-slayer who peaks too early and he finally perishes in a snakepit in Northumbria: the serpents get him in the end.

When they are not eating young girls, dragons have a strange affinity with them, as numerous folktales attest. In the tale of the Dragon of Mordiford in Herefordshire, a green baby wyvern (with wings and two legs), 'scarcely the size of a cucumber', is found in the forest by a little girl called Maud. Her parents know the creature will cause trouble and tell her to return it to the wild. But Maud secretly feeds the wyvern with milk; it grows up to be huge, bright green and capable of flight. Soon it is preying on sheep and cattle, to the despair of local farmers, and when they try to attack it, the dragon develops a taste for human flesh, despite Maud's pleas for it to desist. Eventually the noble young Garston, in full armour, dodges a blast of fire from the beast's gullet and hurls a spear down its throat. Driven insane with grief, Maud mourns her dangerous friend.

In another version, a convict is given the choice between execution and battling the dragon. According to some, he hides in a barrel and when the creature comes down to the River Lugg to drink, the convict fires an arrow through the bunghole and kills it. But the venom spewed out by the dying beast flows into the barrel and kills the convict too. In a more cheerful variant, the convict slays the dragon, cutting out its tongue as proof, and is rewarded with his freedom.

Dragons in Medieval Romance

We tend to imagine the bold knights of medieval romance as doing constant battle with dragons, but in fact these monsters are usually only a rather incidental menace. In one much-imitated tale, Sir Yvain is riding along when he encounters a lion doing battle with a serpentine dragon. Yvain pauses to consider on whose side to intervene; calling up his knowledge of allegory, he reasons that a lion is a noble beast, symbol of kings, while dragons are undoubtedly evil. Yvain consequently slays the dragon and the grateful lion becomes his constant companion, living with him for the rest of his days and joining him in battle against his enemies. Versions of this tale are found widely in European romance: a grateful lion proves a wonderful asset in knightly adventures.

Early in his career, the famous knight Sir Tristan kills a dragon that is menacing the court of the king of Ireland and has slain thousands of knights. Tristan has come to the court to ask for the hand of Princess Iseult for his uncle, King Mark. The king has promised her to whoever can kill the dragon, so Tristan rides out one morning to do battle. Belching smoke, flames and wind, the dragon attacks. Tristan thrusts his spear into the dragon's gaping jaws and gives it a mighty wound. The dragon is not yet fatally injured, so Tristan pursues it and finishes it off with his sword. He cuts out its tongue as proof of his victory and unwisely stuffs it into his clothing for safekeeping. As we know from the bestiaries, the dragon's tongue is highly venomous; exhausted by the battle and the poisonous fumes, Tristan falls unconscious. Meanwhile, the

Serpant

Serphant

Der vochstze

steward of the court, who loves Iseult but who is far too cowardly to face the dragon himself, cuts off the monster's head and carts it back to court to claim his prize. Iseult and her healer-mother find and revive Tristan, and he returns to the court to discover that the steward is demanding Iseult's hand. When Tristan produces the tongue, the sequence of events and the identity of the true victor become clear; Tristan and Iseult depart for Cornwall together. This episode conforms to the widespread 'False Hero' motif of folklore: just when a hero or heroine thinks that success and recognition is within their grasp, another person comes forward to try to snatch the prize from under their noses.

In other romances, facing the dragon may be the last in a series of feats that the hero undertakes to prove himself worthy of a princess's hand, or the first feat that signals an emerging hero, worthy to become a knight. In the romance named after him, Bevis of Hampton does battle with a dragon that, like Fáfnir, was formerly human. There were once two belligerent kings who refused to make peace despite their people's suffering. After death, both are turned into dragons as divine punishment. One of these dragons has now settled near Cologne. Bevis recruits his ally, the pagan giant Ascopard, to help him but Ascopard immediately runs away when he sees the creature. The ensuing battle is recounted at length and in great detail. As in the bestiaries, the dragon's tail proves its most lethal weapon, killing Bevis's horse and cleaving his shield in two.

The story of Sir Tristan and the dragon, from a medieval manuscript of Gottfried von Strassburg's poem *Tristan und Isolde*.

The combat becomes increasingly allegorical; like the Red-Crosse Knight whose story was told earlier, the flagging Bevis is revived by nearby sacred wells and eventually gains victory as much through heartfelt prayer for divine assistance as through his own might.

The author of the Middle English version of *Bevis*, who is responsible for the introduction of the dragon-fight into the story (there is no such battle in his source, written in England, but in French), lists a number of other heroes who also fought dragons: Guy of Warwick, the mysterious figure of Wade, and Sir Lancelot du Lac, who fought against a fire-drake, no less. Lancelot's dragon-killing feats are by no means the climax of his heroic career. In one episode he is menaced by a couple of dragons as he ventures into the Valley of False Lovers, an enchanted domain from which no knight who has ever been untrue to his lady can escape. Lancelot deals with the two creatures easily enough; he enters the castle and breaks the spell, thanks to the power of his unwavering love for Queen Guenevere. Later, Lancelot chances across another dragon guarding the entrance to the castle of Corbenic, where the Holy Grail is to be found. However, this time, it is Lancelot's sinful love for Guenevere, not the power of the monster, that prevents him from achieving the Grail-Quest. These dragons simply constitute yet another obstacle in the hero's path, rather than the ultimate challenge that confirms the superlative courage and skill of the heroic dragon-slayer.

Sir Lancelot du Lac kills a dragon, by Arthur Rackham in the 1917 abridgement of Malory's *Morte D'Arthur, The Romance of King Arthur and His Knights.*

The Lambton Worm

Some dragons in British tradition have unusual origins. The famous Lambton Worm of County Durham is one such. A little eel-like creature was fished up by John Lambton, the heir to the Lambton estate, when he skipped church one Sunday to go fishing in the River Wear. The creature seems sinister to John, so he throws it down a nearby well. Years pass, and John goes off to the Crusades. Meanwhile, the locals realise that a worm has arrived in the neighbourhood: the well has become poisonous and the monster is devouring local cattle and children. It would 'swally little bairns alive / when they laid doon te sleep', according to a nineteenth-century pantomime song. Soon it takes up residence near the Lambton castle; John's father appeases it by giving it the milk of nine cows every day, but this is not a situation that can be sustained for long. At last John returns and resolves to rid the community of this nuisance. Taking the advice of a witch who reveals his responsibility for its origins and who warns that after killing the creature he must then kill the first living creature he sees, John does battle with the fearsome monster by the side of the Wear. At the witch's prompting, John obtains special armour with protruding spear-heads. When the worm wraps itself around him to strangle him in its snaky coils it cuts itself to pieces, which wash away in the river; normally the worm's severed sections would come together and reconstitute the monster. John has agreed with his father to send out his favourite hunting hound at a pre-arranged signal, but the father is so excited when he knows the dragon is dead, he rushes out to greet his son. John, quite properly, refuses

The Lambton Worm devours a goose, illustrated by Herbert Cole in the 1906 collection *Fairy-Gold: A Book of Old English Fairy Tales*.

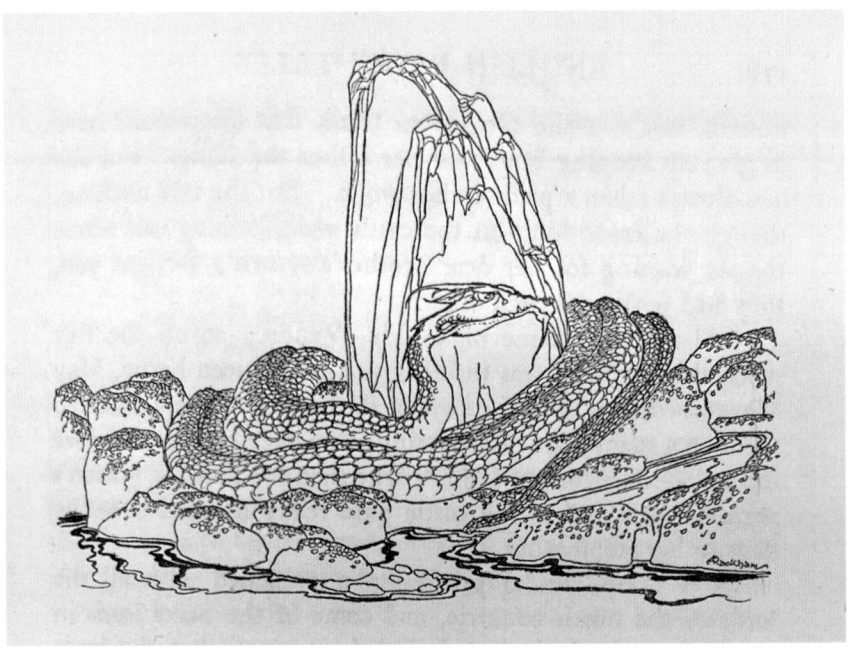

The Laidly Worm of Spindleston Heugh, illustrated by Arthur Rackham in *English Fairy Tales Retold* by F. A. Steel.

to kill his own father, and does indeed slay the dog. Nevertheless, he has called down a curse upon himself: that nine generations of Lambtons should not die peacefully in their beds.

This dragon is generated by antisocial behaviour. John's decision to go fishing instead of attending church is compounded by throwing the strange creature into a communal water source. The connection between dragons and water supplies is an ancient one, as seen in the Greek myths noted above. The Lambton Worm legend was the basis for Bram Stoker's second most famous horror novel, *The Lair of the White Worm*, published in 1911. In this book just such a child-snatching worm terrorises a neighbourhood in Derbyshire, devouring children. The worm is destroyed by a combination of divine justice (a huge thunderstorm) and modern technology (a wire and dynamite) which explodes the monster once and for all.

Loathly Worms and Enchanted Girls

The Laidly Worm of Spindleston Heugh is another monster from north-east England. The widowed king, who lives in Bamburgh castle, takes a second wife; she is beautiful, but also a witch. The king's son has journeyed overseas, but his daughter Margaret remains at home. Lady Margaret is so lovely that her stepmother becomes jealous of her and turns her into a 'laidly [loathly] worm.' The monster lurks in a cave near the crag of Spindleston Heugh, devouring seven cows a day. Her brother, Child Wynd, returns from abroad and vows to deal with the creature. Realising the dragon's true identity, Child Wynd kisses it rather than trying to slaughter it. Margaret is restored to her rightful form and the witch-queen is deservedly turned into a toad. This tale, recorded in a folksong from 1778, has affinities with other older ballads, such as that of Allison Gross. Allison is similarly turned into a worm; in her case, three kisses from the hero are required to disenchant her.

The motif of the *fier baiser* or 'proud kiss' is widespread in European romance. The knight encounters a female dragon-like monster and is challenged to kiss it; he must overcome his fear and disgust in order to approach the beast. In one fifteenth-century Venetian tale, Sir Galvano (Gawain) encounters La Ponzela Gaia in dragon-shape. She is in fact the daughter of the enchantress Morgan le Fay, who seems to have bewitched her in order to preserve her virginity. Galvano and the serpent fight, but when he reveals his name she turns into a beautiful girl and they quickly become lovers.

Not every knight has Gawain's courtly reputation and courage. In a story related in the fourteenth-century *Travels of Sir John Mandeville*, King Ypocras' daughter, who rules over the island of Lango, near Crete, has been turned by the goddess Diana into a dragon, a hundred fathoms long. The dragon lives in a cave and does no harm. She can be disenchanted by a kiss, and a knight from Rhodes vows to break the spell. But when he sees the monster he turns and flees, and the enraged dragon dashes him against a rock and kills him. Another man chances across the girl in her human form and she explains how to rescue her. The man returns next day but when he sees her dragon form, 'so hideous and horrible', he too flees onto his ship, pursued by the monster who laments piteously. The man dies while the poor dragon is still waiting for the right hero to break the spell. This lovelorn figure reminds us of Dragon in the *Shrek* movie franchise, a female dragon who is also hoping for love. Dragon becomes an ally rather than an enemy, swallowing up the evil Lord Farquaad and – in an unusual interspecies move – marrying Shrek's sidekick, Donkey, and becoming the mother of dragon–donkey hybrids.

The Dragon of Wantley

An emerging pattern in worm-type dragon stories is that the older heroic attack with sword, lance or spear, undertaken by an aristocratic young man, is displaced by tales in which an often low-born hero, like the Mordiford convict, conquers the beast through cunning and applied technology (Sigurd's pit-ambush can be assigned to this category). Spiked armour, poisoned bait and even – as we will see in 'Water-Dragons and Sea-Serpents' – buckets of flaming peat are effective against individual dragons.

The legend of the Dragon of Wantley features a noble (in rank, if not in moral character) and a talking monster. While the scientific rationalism of the Enlightenment concluded that the dragon could not be classified within the emerging discipline of zoology, indeed did not actually exist, the popular parodic tale of the Dragon of Wantley relegated the monster to a purely comic foe. The story first appears in a comic broadside of 1685, and tells how the dragon, almost as big as the Trojan Horse, not only ate up cattle and sheep and three children, but also started to devour whole forests and buildings. 'Burning snivel' runs from the creature's nose, which he directs into a nearby well so that it looks like a 'brook of burning brandy'. The desperate community turns to the dissolute local nobleman, More of More Hall. The price he demands for his services is the attentions of a maid of sixteen, 'brisk and keen', who will 'anoint' him all night before battle, then dress him in his custom-made spiked armour of Sheffield steel, which made him look 'like an Egyptian porcupig'. Having fortified himself with

Sheet music for the comic opera *The Dragon of Wantley*, illustrated in George Bickham's *The Musical Entertainer*.

strong drink, More hides down a well and springs out, crying 'boo', when the dragon comes to drink. The annoyed dragon turns round and defecates over him. Now they join in combat and wrestle fiercely. In dire straits, More manages to free himself and delivers a mighty kick to the dragon's 'arse-gut' with his spiked boot. 'Alack,

alack', the dragon laments, 'had you but mist that place / You could have done me no mischief', and with that, he expires.

The tale was adapted in 1737 as a comic opera, with a libretto by Henry Carey and music by the German-born John Frederick Lampe. Satirising the excesses of contemporary opera, pastiching both Italian opera and the work of George Frederick Handel, the show had its debut at the Haymarket Theatre and then transferred to Covent Garden for a very long run indeed. It was here that Handel saw and praised the opera, for its composer was a bassoonist in his orchestra. Something of the tenor of the piece can be gauged from such lines as 'What wretched Havock does this dragon make!', 'What nasty Dog has got in the well / Disturbed my drink and made the water smell' and 'Oh! The Devil take your toe!', with which the dragon expires. *The Dragon of Wantley* was one of the most successful theatrical productions of the eighteenth century, but that very popularity made it hard for dragons to be taken seriously for a good hundred years or more. 'No dragon could be brought before the public without ridicule', noted the naturalist William John Broderip in 1849. Thus, we find stories recorded in the twentieth century such as the 'Dragon of Filey Brigg' in which a dragon is undone by its taste for the sticky Yorkshire gingerbread, parkin, and the tale of the Knucker of Sussex recounted later; comic dragons became a staple in children's fiction.

thesauros in celo. ubi neq; erugo. neq; tinea demolitur
& ubi fures ñ effodiunt nec furantur. Tinea ū que ue
stes corrodit latent. designat inuidiā que studiū bonū
lacerat & cōparationē unitatis demoliri ñ cessat. Fu
res nāq; demones atq; heretici ꝼ de quibꝯ ūitas atꝯ. Oms
qꝗquot uenerūt. fures sunt & latrones.

WATER-DRAGONS AND SEA-SERPENTS

We have already met the Leviathan, the dragon-snake of the Bible whom God is said to have fought in the Book of Isaiah, and Jörmungandr, the Norse World-Serpent who will battle against the god Thor at *ragna rök*. The Loch Ness Monster is not normally thought of as a dragon, but he or she may indeed be such a beast. The Loch Ness Monster is first heard of, not in the loch itself, but nearby, in Adomnán's *Life of Saint Columba*, from around 700 CE. Columba is travelling near the loch when he hears that a water-monster has eaten a man. One of his disciples swims in the River Ness to draw the creature out; when it emerges, ready to devour him, the sign of the Cross drives it away, if only as far as the loch. However, there are no further attested monster sightings before the late nineteenth century, so clearly Columba had some success in his banishment. The Loch Ness Monster has many relatives across the world. The *mokele-mbembe* of the Congo (possibly a reminiscence of a kind of rhinoceros) and the Lagarfljót Worm in

Aquatic monsters and sea-dragons from a medieval bestiary.

eastern Iceland, Bessie the monster of Lake Erie and the Australian Bunyip, who haunts billabongs, are just some of these water-dwelling reptiles.

Merlin and the Dragons

In Arthurian legend, two water-dragons, one red and one white, make a thorough nuisance of themselves in the mountains of North Wales. Here Vortigern, the tyrannical High King of Britain, is building a mighty tower, but every night the earth shakes and the tower tumbles down. Vortigern's advisers tell him that the problem can be solved by sacrificing a boy who has no father, and his men locate one such in South Wales. This is the boy Merlin, whose mother is a princess and whose father is unknown, even to her (it turns out that Merlin's father was a demon). When Merlin is brought to the spot, he laughs at the wisdom of the advisers. Do they know what lies beneath the tower? Digging reveals a subterranean lake. And do they know what lies below the lake? The advisers do not, but Merlin does. When the lake is drained the red and white dragons are revealed; they fight one another every night and their combat is what makes the tower fall down. Merlin is vindicated and Vortigern puts his counsellors to death for their ignorance. Geoffrey of Monmouth, who is the first to tell this story in his *History of the Kings of Britain* from around 1138, does not relate what happens to the dragons nor to Vortigern's

The tyrannical King Vortigern depicted with the red and white dragons in a medieval manuscript.

e donne un riche dun naal petris
i uns des dragons est tote blance
t li autre est rouge q bénus
i Rois sist grent salozer
t le siure mesdisiet
dragons sunt del siure saillir
t forement des sunt en vage
ar grant sierte contre saillerent
i ke li betroy tot les virent
ien les reiles esdouuer
t des goules flambes ietter

building project. Soon the news comes that Uther Pendragon, father of King Arthur, is advancing against the King and Vortigern is overthrown. The white dragon comes to represent the invading Saxons, while the red dragon stands first for Uther, and then for the indigenous Celts who resist the English, and indeed remains to this day the symbol of Wales.

The Mester Stoor Worm

The Mester Stoor Worm was a sea-dragon, living in the waters of the Orkney Isles, who ate seven girls every Saturday. Finally, a poor and unregarded lad called Assipattle rowed out to meet him with a bucket containing burning peats in his boat. The dragon opened its huge jaws and swallowed Assipattle along with his bucket. The dragon's liver caught fire from the peats; in its death throes it spewed up Assipattle and split apart. The dragon's teeth became the Faroe Islands; its torso, still smouldering, became the volcanic terrain of Iceland. Assipattle's name relates him to Scandinavian ne'er-do-well folk heroes who prefer to lie in the ashes on the hearth than do useful work around the farm; as reward for his courage he marries the king's daughter.

The Sussex Knucker

In addition to the two mighty dragons in *Beowulf* whom we've already met, there is an episode where Beowulf is tracking the monstrous figure of Grendel's mother. Beowulf has already killed her terrifying man-eating son, and must now eliminate the mother who has taken vengeance for her child's death. The mere beneath which she lives is a strange and uncanny place. At night flames burn on its surface, hoar-frost glints on the trees that overhang it, and basking on its rocky shoreline are 'sædracas' and 'nicoras', water-dragons and nickers, a type of water-monster that can take different forms. The Knucker (an alternative spelling for 'nicker') in this folktale dwells deep in a pond at Lyminster in Sussex, from which it emerges to devour cattle. The King of Sussex promises his daughter to whoever can eliminate the beast; in an older account a knight turns up and kills it in the usual way. But there's an alternative version, recorded in the early twentieth century, in which Jim Puttock, an ingenious local lad, makes a huge suet pudding and carts it to Knucker Hole, the pond where the dragon lives. The dragon pokes its head out of the water.

'What you got there?' says Dragon, sniffing.
'Pudden', says Jim.
'Pudden?' says Dragon. 'What be that?'
'Just you try', says Jim.

The dragon swallows up horse, cart, pudding and all, and sinks to the bottom of Knucker Hole, never to be seen again. In another version the Knucker demands a second pudding. When this excess gives him the 'collywobbles', Jim offers to help alleviate his stomach-ache, but whips out an axe and chops off his head instead.

aūt Georgi martir ̄icl̄ite te decet
laus' et gl̄a ̄sootatu militia per

SAINTS AND DRAGONS

Saints have their own particular methods for dealing with dragons, which (apart from the two soldier-saints, George and Theodore) do not involve their slaying the beasts. Saints are usually called in when dragons are causing the usual kinds of trouble: marauding in the neighbourhood, devouring cattle and humans, or refusing access to local water sources. The monsters often have toxic breath that poisons the water, or creates a miasma that slays everything close to their lairs.

One of the earliest recorded saintly dragon-tales is that of St Thomas, the Apostle of India. Thomas comes across the corpse of a handsome young man and prays over it. As he does so, a huge black dragon emerges from a hole in the ground and explains that he had fallen in love with a beautiful young woman in the neighbourhood; this young man was the girl's lover. The dragon has killed him out of jealousy and, furthermore, because the couple had had sex on the Sabbath. The dragon claims kinship with the Devil and reels off a series of crimes for which he or his kindred

Illumination of St George slaying the dragon and rescuing the princess, from the sixteenth-century Hours of Joanna I of Castile.

have been responsible, including the slaying of Abel and Judas's betrayal. Thomas commands the dragon to suck the poison from the boy's wound. The young man revives, but the dragon bursts into pieces, destroyed by ingesting its own toxin. The young man and a multitude of others convert to Christianity after this demonstration of God's power; that the dragon confesses his diabolical heritage means that his explosive end is well deserved.

A variant dragon-legend from the West of England is that of St Carantoc. A holy man from Cardigan in South Wales, Carantoc is the king's son, but prefers the life of a hermit. When his father dies, the people try to force him to take the throne, so he flees across the River Severn. He loses his stone altar in the crossing, but it is found washed up near Carhampton in Somerset where Carantoc intends to found a monastery. When he requests permission from King Arthur, Arthur asks him first to deal with a troublesome dragon who lives in the marshes, vanishing under the surface every time the king and his entourage try to attack. Carantoc prays for God's help and the dragon emerges, bowing its head. Carantoc puts his priestly stole around the dragon's neck and leads it away to the hall of another local ruler, where he proposes that it might be kept as a pet. When the king's followers want instead to kill it, Carantoc argues that the dragon is one of God's creatures like any other, put into the world to terrify sinners and to signify God's power. Then he releases the beast, commanding it to go far away and do no further harm. And away the dragon goes, never to be heard of again. Carantoc's method of dealing with dragons seems a humane and ecologically sensitive interpretation; his reading of the dragon as just another member of God's creation rather than a proxy for the Devil enables the creature to retreat to the wilderness where it no longer harms humans.

Female Saints and Dragons

In heroic tradition, women do not take up weapons against dragons, but female saints can harness the power of God just as effectively as any man. St Martha, the sister of Mary of Bethany and Lazarus, whom Jesus raised from the dead, took ship along with other believers across the Mediterranean after the ascension of Christ into heaven. They landed in the south of France, where they set about converting the people. In the River Rhône, between Arles and Avignon, there lurked a terrible dragon called Tarasconus. Sometimes described as a hybrid monster, with a lion's head, a serpent's tail, teeth and horns, Tarasconus is consistently referred to as a dragon. The creature made a habit of sinking the ships that sailed along the Rhône and devouring their crew. At the request of the local inhabitants, Martha went in search of the beast and discovered him eating a man in the forest by the river. She threw holy water over Tarasconus and confronted him with a wooden cross. The monster stood stock still 'like a sheep', says the *Golden Legend* account, and the saint bound him with her girdle; the people then attacked and killed the beast. The Provençal town of Tarascon takes its name from Tarasconus. Martha's feat in overcoming the dragon is celebrated annually with a procession through the town and a re-enactment of the monster's death.

𝔈 Adonay thi imperator celorum huiusme hostes

St Margaret triumphs over a demonic dragon, as depicted in a fifteenth-century Book of Hours.

Opposite: St Martha and the dragon Tarasconus, as they appear in a fifteenth-century French manuscript.

A rather different dragon-tale is told of St Margaret of Antioch, known in the Eastern Orthodox Church as St Marina. Margaret converted to Christianity as a child and was disowned by her father. She was living as a shepherdess when the pagan governor of the Diocese of the East decided he wanted to marry her, demanding that she renounce her faith. Margaret refused and was subjected to various tortures. Locked up in a prison cell, she was alarmed when a demon in the form of a dragon appeared. It had a crest and beard of gold and went, so it said, by the name of Rouphos. The flames the dragon was belching lit up the dark cell and he swallowed Margaret whole. Yet such was the power of Margaret's prayer within the monster that the dragon's belly burst open and she stepped out unharmed with a cross in her hand. It is no surprise that, as the patron saint of childbirth, she should be invoked to help with pregnancy and the safe delivery of babies. In the Middle Ages, birthing girdles, ornamented with images of Margaret or tiny written accounts of her victory, were bound round the woman in labour to secure a speedy and successful release of the child within.

Theodore and George

The original saintly dragon-killer was not St George, but St Theodore Tiro, martyred in the third or early fourth century. He is first definitely depicted as killing a dragon in a tenth-century image, and a statue of Theodore killing a crocodile can be seen on a pillar in St Mark's Square in Venice, for Theodore was the city's first patron saint before St Mark displaced him. Subsequently the dragon-slaying legend became attributed to George, up until that point just another martyr. In the Eastern Church, the two saints are often pictured together, mounted on horses and slaying dragons, symbolising the Church overcoming evil. Rather like Perseus with Andromeda, George happens across Princess Sabra. Her name has

An Ethiopian miniature of St George slaying the dragon, from a
seventeenth-century manuscript The Four Gospels.

been drawn by lot and she is about to be fed to a dragon whose lair
is near the city of Silene, in Libya. George first wounds, then tames
the dragon through the sign of the Cross, such that the princess can
lead it along with her girdle, 'as a meek beast and debonair', says
William Caxton's translation of the story. The princess, the knight
and the dragon return to Silene where George demands that the
people convert to Christianity, or he will unleash the creature. Only
once they are baptised does he draw his sword and smite off the
dragon's head. The stories of Theodore and George thus conform to
the types found in the ancient Near East and in classical legend: the
hero slays the chaos-monster and brings safety – and salvation – to
the folk whom the monster had menaced.

DRAGONS FROM AROUND THE WORLD

Chinese and other Asian dragons have already been mentioned. In Chinese lore, the *long* or *loong* is snake-like; it has four legs with huge claws, and it sports impressive whiskers and horns. Traditionally, the dragon lives in rivers, but it was also a long-standing symbol of imperial power. The five-clawed dragon motif could only be used by the emperor himself, while the four-clawed dragon was reserved for imperial family members. The Chinese dragon is a creature of prosperity and good fortune and is associated with positive *qi* energy. The Dragon-God brings rain, though too much rain, causing flooding, can be brought about by hostile dragon figures. The dragon's enemy is the tiger and they are often depicted in combat together. Although they are not winged, these dragons can fly; as they pass through the air they presage storms and rain.

Embroidered roundel from an imperial robe of the Ming dynasty, depicting the imperial Chinese five-clawed dragon.

Japanese myths tell of an eight-headed and eight-tailed giant serpent who was killed by the god Susanowo, who thereby gained the famous sword Kusanagi no Tsurugi, still part of the Japanese imperial regalia. More typical is Ryūo, the god of the sea, who is often known as the Dragon-King. In one well-known tale a man called Urashima rescues a turtle who is being tormented by children. Later a beautiful woman appears to him; she is the Dragon-King's daughter. She had in fact been the turtle whom he rescued, and she invites Urashima to live with her in the undersea kingdom. The couple are very happy but after a while Urashima misses his parents and home. He is given leave to visit, but when he returns to his village, everyone he knows is dead, for time runs differently under the waves. In desperation he opens a box which his wife had given him; this turns him into an old man and he dies peacefully as a human should, refusing his chance of immortality.

Like Chinese dragons, Japanese and Korean dragons are also associated with river spirits. In Hayao Miyazaki's animated film *Spirited Away*, from 2001, the good witch Zeniba declares, 'All dragons are kind. Kind and stupid' – the complete opposite of the Western dragons we have met. The dragon to whom Zeniba refers is a splendid white creature, a form assumed by Haku, apprentice to the wicked witch Yubaba and ally of the film's heroine, Chihiro. At the end of the film Haku is revealed to be the spirit of a river into which Chihiro had once fallen as a toddler, creating a connection between them that survives into the spirit world.

Painting on silk of a dragon and a tiger by Shen Quan, from the Qing dynasty.

The Japanese god Susanowo killing the eight-headed dragon, in a print by Torii Kiyomasu III, 1748.

Opposite: The dragon-king Ryūo and his daughter bid farewell to Urashima as he returns home from the underwater palace, print by Tsukioka Yoshitoshi, 1886.

In Slavic countries, Russia in particular, the many-headed dragon is rife. Gorynych is a mighty three-headed serpent who swims in the Puchai river, which separates this world from the Other World. The hero Dobrynya Nikitin swims in the river; the pair fight and the dragon agrees to leave Russia alone if Dobrynya will keep out of the river in future. The dragon keeps his word with regard to Russia but flies instead to Kyiv and abducts the niece of Prince Vladimir. Dobrynya effects a rescue, overcoming the beast with a 'Greek cap' (probably a monastic hood); a princess and many other captives are liberated. Gorynych thus represents the enemies of Russia, overcome by heroic courage and the power of the Orthodox Church. Another Russian dragon, Tugarin, has paper wings; his adversary prays for rain which successfully grounds the beast as his wings collapse. The Wawel dragon of the Polish city of Kraków is also multi-headed and a great devourer of people and cattle. An ingenious cobbler called Skuba overcomes it with a lamb carcass stuffed with sulphur. The sulphur gives the dragon an extraordinary thirst and it drinks so much water from the River Vistula that it explodes. Skuba marries the king's daughter and lives happily ever after.

The creation myths of various Australian Aboriginal peoples often make reference to the Serpent or Rainbow Serpent. This being creates land and brings order out of primordial chaos, but if disturbed or offended it can unleash chaos once again. The serpent goes by many names, though it is often identified with the rainbow. Its home is in a huge water-hole, but it often moves between smaller ones, showing humans where they can find this precious resource. In some traditions it falls from the sky or arises from the depths of the earth, and its thrashing creates mountains, valleys and plains.

In ancient Mexico the dragon is one aspect of Quetzalcoatl, the Feathered Serpent of Aztec and Mayan myth. This figure is associated with the creation of humans and was the god of wind; when the weather was stormy, Quetzalcoatl was said to be angry.

Gorynych, the three-headed serpent, defeated by the Russian folk-hero Dobrynya Nikitin, illustrated by Ivan Bilibin.

Conversation with Smaug

CONTEMPORARY DRAGONS

By the late nineteenth century, dragons had been relegated to appearances in children's stories. But with the rediscovery of *Beowulf*, and the popularity of Wagner's *Ring*, with its complex depiction of Fafner, his name for Fáfnir, dragons began to be taken more seriously. Smaug, Tolkien's immensely dangerous dragon, combining traits of the Beowulfian fire-drake with the ability to speak like Fáfnir, is the first of many significant dragons. In one of C. S. Lewis's Narnia stories, *The Voyage of the Dawn Treader* (1952), the selfish and greedy Eustace Scrubb transforms into a dragon when he puts on a gold bracelet he discovers in a dragon's lair: 'Sleeping on a dragon's hoard with greedy, dragonish thoughts in his heart, he had become a dragon himself,' says the narrator. As Lewis's Narnia series is consistently allegorical, it is unsurprising that the sin of avarice should manifest itself in dragon form. At first Eustace is quite pleased to be huge and terrifying, but when he realises he is now bereft of friends he becomes repentant. Thus,

Smaug as he appears in the first edition of J. R. R Tolkien's *The Hobbit*, 1937.

Aslan, the Christ-like lion of the series, can now come to him. Through a watery ceremony that is analogous to baptism, Aslan claws off Eustace's dragon-skin and restores him to human form, a better person for his experience.

Ursula Le Guin's Earthsea series features flying and talking dragons who are old, wise and speak in the ancient language of the Making. Wizards can commune with dragons and, if they know the dragon's true name, can control them, preventing them from attacking humans in search of food or gold. These dragons have razor-sharp teeth, but do not breathe fire. Two of the most significant dragons in the sequence are named Orm and Orm Embar – the Old Norse term for dragon, as we saw above. Earthsea's dragons are extremely long-lived and therefore wise; their knowledge far exceeds that of humans and they are neither good nor evil. Orm Embar, indeed, gives his life to destroy the evil wizard Cob, whose existence endangers the world of Earthsea.

We saw above how the dragons of *Game of Thrones* are descended via Tolkien's Smaug from the Beowulfian fire-drake. They are the ultimate weapon in a dangerous world, endowing their riders with enormous strategic power and demonstrating how easily such power becomes tyrannical. Dragons are a blunt instrument; dragonfire is not discriminating when unleashed in rage and the problem of feeding the beasts is a perennial one. One of Daenerys

Still from Studio Ghibli's animated film *Tales from Earthsea* (2006), based on Ursula K. Le Guin's Earthsea series.

A replica of a dragon from the *Game of Thrones* television show, on display at the 2019 Comic Con in Warsaw, Poland.

Stormborn's dragons, Drogon, causes consternation when it fails to distinguish between a goat and the young child tending the herd when it is out hunting; on a larger scale, Drogon later destroys the entire city of King's Landing.

Not all modern dragons are quite so terrifying. 'Puff the Magic Dragon', a poignant song composed in 1962 by Peter Yarrow, of the group Peter, Paul and Mary, tells of a friendly dragon called Puff whose friend is a child called Jackie Paper. They have adventures together, sailing the high seas and fighting pirates. But Jackie grows too old to believe in dragons and stops visiting his friend, and Puff is left to mourn alone in his cave. The song reached number two in the US charts when it was released and has been covered by many singers in different languages: Marlene Dietrich sings a notable German version. At one point it was claimed that the song contained coded references to drug-taking, a rumour roundly rejected by the song's composer, who maintained that it was about the loss of childhood innocence and imagination.

The British children's writer Cressida Cowell created a hugely popular series called How to Train Your Dragon, published from 2003. Set in a fantasy Viking world, the stories relate how a young Viking lad called Hiccup Horrendous Haddock the Third trains the dragon Toothless to be his hunting-dragon and what happens thereafter. Hiccup, a clever lad, speaks Dragonese and becomes a great hero, despite being thought unpromising in his younger days. Numerous other dragons appear in the series; some even stage a dragon rebellion, leading to a climactic dragon-versus -Viking battle. The book series is now complete, but a Dreamworks media franchise has continued to produce original stories about these dragons and their world. Younger readers are familiar with Zog the dragon, created in 2010 by writer Julia Donaldson and illustrator Axel Scheffler. Zog is a young, somewhat accident-prone dragon who tries very hard in dragon school to become a good and effective dragon.

Illustration of Puff the Magic Dragon and Jackie Paper by John Shelley.

CONCLUSION

We may all think we know what a dragon is, and what it symbolises, but as we have seen, the form and function of dragons have been changeable over the centuries and across the world. In the West they are frightening and evil, especially when roused. They crave gold which they hoard rather than letting it circulate for the common good; they destroy the environment and make life unliveable for their neighbours, wreaking social and economic destruction. They may be demonic, the Devil in bestial form, but alternatively they may just be another strange kind of animal, like the whale or the elephant. Parts of these actual dragons can be used, with expert knowledge, as medicine, proving that God has created them for his own inscrutable purposes. Not every dragon is content with its condition; for every Fáfnir, sitting smugly on his hoard, there is a bewitched woman, suffering agonies of anticipation as she hopes desperately for rescue.

Slaying the dragon is the ultimate heroic feat, a battle that often lasts for days and where victory can sometimes be won only with God's help. Sword and spear, along with effective armour, may be enough for the noble hero; other dragon-fighters use fire or poison, turning the creature's capabilities back against itself. Not all dragons must be annihilated. St Carantoc's tale suggests that there should be space for dragons in our world, as long as they present no threat to human habitats. How we read dragons is not a straightforward matter; a symbol of horror and evil for centuries in the West, they became regarded as comic and childish in the modern era before once again coming to signify weapons of mass destruction, particularly those used in aerial warfare.

Elsewhere in the world, the dragon has a more positive significance. It is still a creature of enormous power, but a power that can be harnessed for good, to bring rain to make crops grow, to create and shape our environment, and even to bring humans themselves into existence. Their association with snakes connotes access to hidden wisdom; they have knowledge of what lies buried within the earth, whether that be precious gold or ancient secrets. Over the centuries dragons have proved to be remarkable and enduring creatures in our collective imaginary, inviting us to think about what is valuable, what is worth fighting for or against, and the nature of the hostile powers that are ranged against us.

Overleaf: Illustration by Henry Justice Ford of the Red-Crosse Knight and Una standing over the vanquished dragon, from *The Red Romance Book* edited by Andrew Lang.

THE END O

DRAGON

Picture Credits